P9-CQJ-374

SCAREDY
MOUSE

For Annie
~A. M.

For the Farmhouse Mice
~T. W.

tiger tales
5 River Road, Suite 128, Wilton, CT 06897
Published in the United States 2019
Originally published in Great Britain 2002
by Little Tiger Press Ltd.

Visit Tim Warnes at www.ChapmanandWarnes.com
ISBN-13: 978-1-68010-162-1
ISBN-10: 1-68010-162-5
Printed in China
LTP/1400/2626/0219

10 9 8 7 6 5 4 3 2 1

For more insight and activities, visit us at
www.tigertalesbooks.com

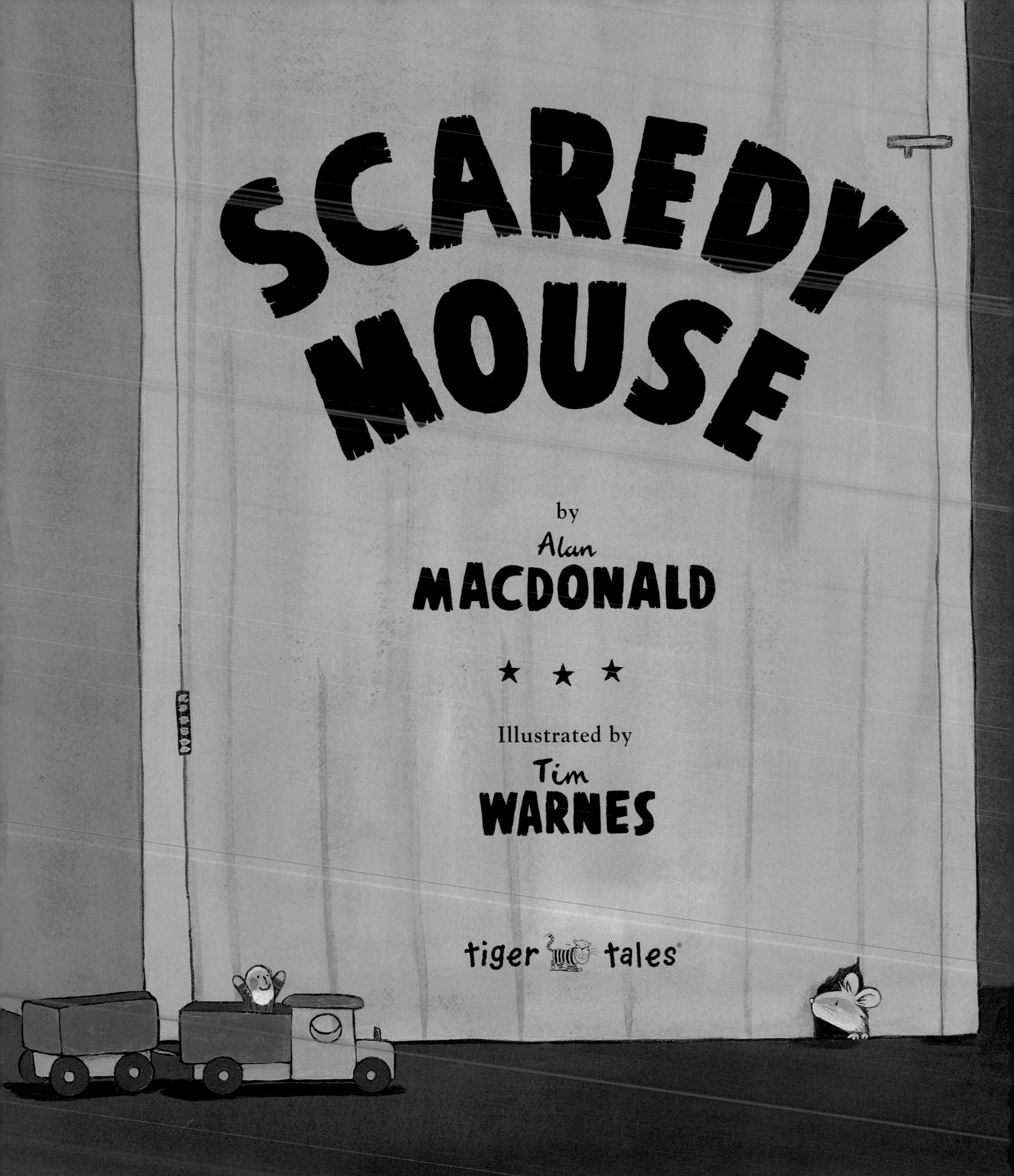

SCAREDY MOUSE

by

Alan MACDONALD

★ ★ ★

Illustrated by

Tim WARNES

tiger tales®

In a small hole behind a
cupboard under the stairs lived
a large family of mice.
The youngest was named Squeak.
Squeak was a small mouse,
a scaredy mouse,
a stay-at-home mouse.

One evening, Squeak was woken up by his sister, Nibbles.

"Let's go to the kitchen," she said. "I just saw something yummy. A chocolate cake as big as a wheel."

Squeak loved chocolate, but he was very scared.

"What if I get lost?" he worried. "What if we meet the big orange cat with green eyes?"

"The orange cat is asleep," said Nibbles. "And I know how to keep you from getting lost."

Nibbles found a big ball of string and tied one end around Squeak. "There," she said. "All you have to do is follow the string, and you'll find your way home."

They scurried out of the mousehole and into the dark, shadowy hall. Squeak stayed close to Nibbles, trailing the string behind him. But as they crossed the hall, Squeak saw a long, striped tail.

"IT'S THE CAT,
IT'S THE CAT!"
he cried.
Squeak ran this way and that way,
here and there, around and back.
"Don't be scared," said Nibbles . . . .

Squeak slowly came out of his hiding place.

Nibbles and Squeak scampered through the living room, under the table and under the chairs. But just as Squeak was about to eat a cookie crumb, he saw two eyes gleaming in the dark.

"IT'S THE CAT,
IT'S THE CAT!"
he cried.
Squeak ran this way and that way,
here and there, around and back.
"Don't be scared," said Nibbles . . . .

Squeak smiled nervously.

They crept into the living room, past the fireplace and past the ticking clock.

Suddenly, Squeak froze in his tracks. There, peeking above the arm of the chair, was a head with two pointy ears.

"IT'S THE CAT, IT'S THE CAT!"
he cried.
Squeak ran this way and that way,
here and there, around and back.
"Don't be scared," said Nibbles . . . .

"Oh, good!" said Squeak.

The two mice tiptoed into the kitchen, across the floor and past the cupboard. Squeak peeked inside.

He shivered and shook. There, in the shadows, was something furry.

"IT'S THE CAT,
IT'S THE CAT!"
he cried.
Squeak ran this way
and that way,
here and there,
around and back.
"Don't be scared,"
said Nibbles . . . .

"Phew!" sighed Squeak.

Just then, Nibbles spotted the chocolate cake on top of the refrigerator. It didn't take them long to find their way up to it. Soon their paws and whiskers were sticky with chocolate.

"Yum," sighed Nibbles.
"I could eat all day."
Squeak was a hungry mouse,
but also a worried mouse,
a scaredy mouse,
a want-to-go-home mouse.

So Nibbles scrambled
down the refrigerator . . .

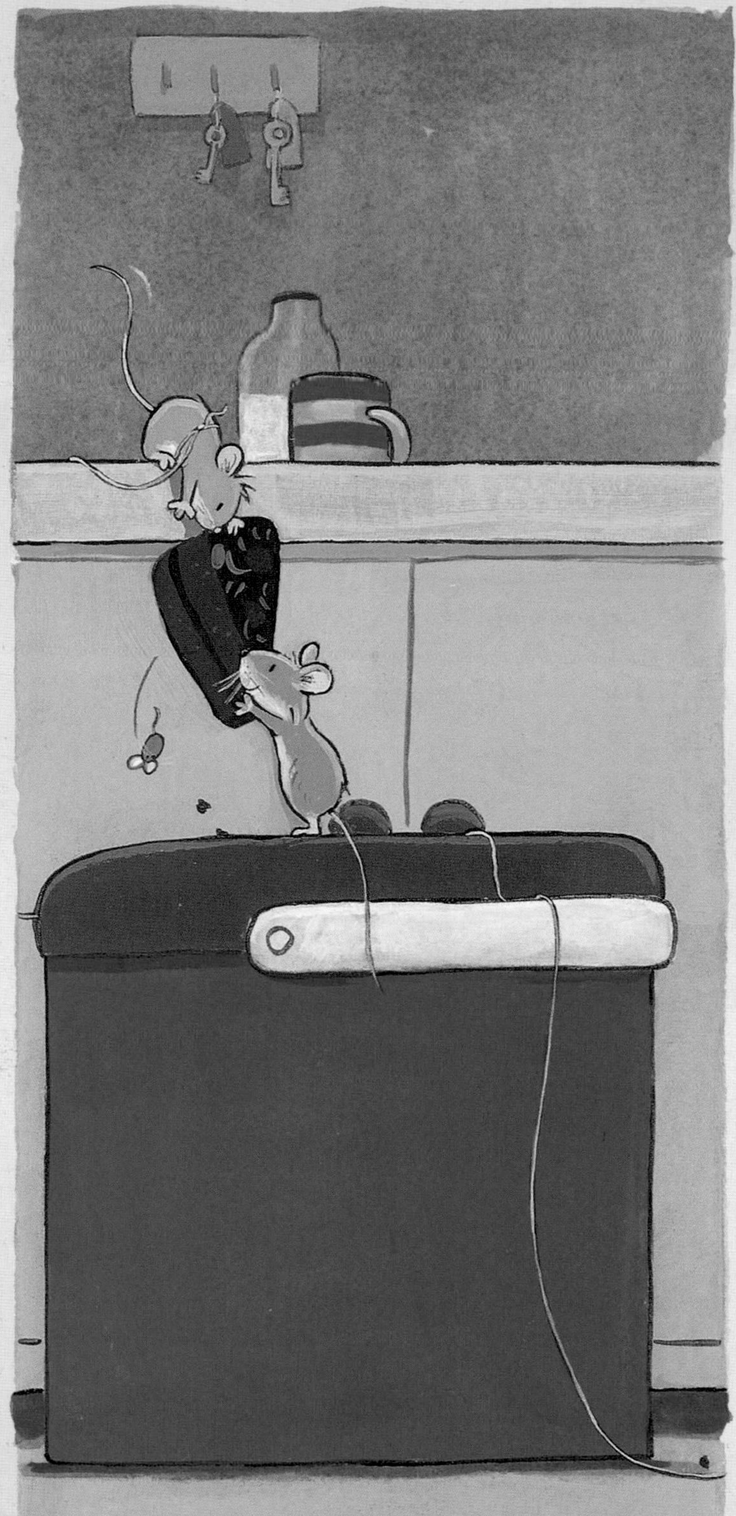

and Squeak and the
cake followed.

They heaved the cake across the
floor, but just as they reached the door,
a shadow fell across their path.
"IT'S THE CAT, IT'S THE CAT!"
cried Squeak.
“Don’t be scared,” said Nibbles.
“It’s only . . .”

THE CAT!
Run, Squeak!

Squeak ran this way and that way,
here and there, around and back.
The big orange cat narrowed his
eyes, opened his claws, and . . .

. . . pounced.

But the cat found himself caught in a web of string. The more he struggled, the more he became tangled up . . .

until he was tied
up just like a big
orange package.

Squeak was no longer a scaredy mouse. He was a bold-as-a-lion mouse.

And the next time he met the big orange cat, he just said . . .

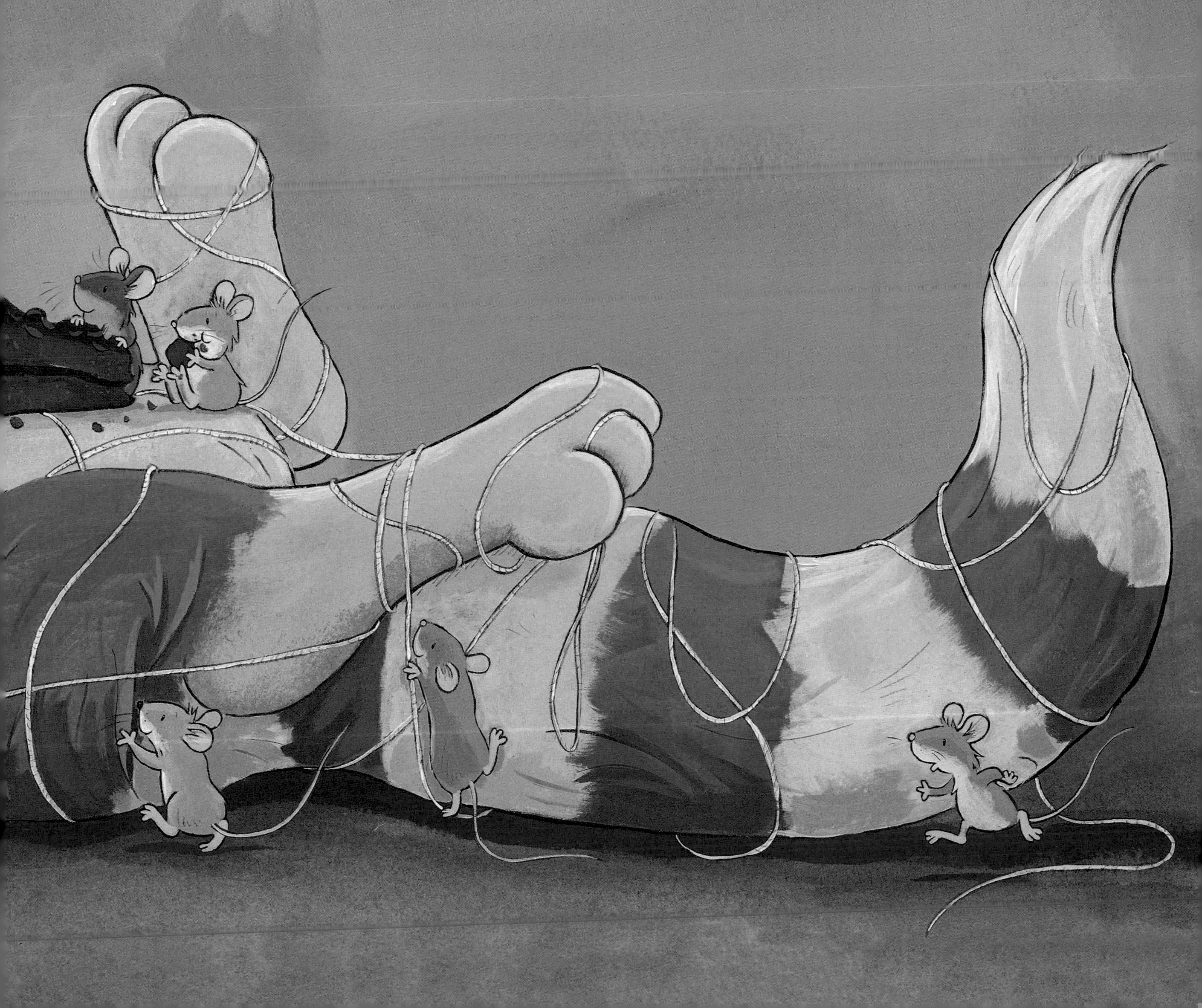

BOO!

Alan MacDonald

Alan dreamed of becoming a professional soccer player, but when he won a pen in a writing competition, his fate was sealed. He has written more than 80 children's books, which have been translated into many languages and have won several awards. Alan also writes for TV.

Tim Warnes

Award-winning illustrator Tim Warnes shares a studio at his home in Dorset in England with his wife, illustrator Jane Chapman. Tim is best known for illustrating the Little Tiger books, which gave Little Tiger Press not only its name, but its first ever logo, too!